Parents and Caregivers,

Stone Arch Readers are designed to provide enjoyable reading experiences, as well as opportunities to develop vocabulary, literacy skills, and comprehension. Here are a few ways to support your beginning reader:

• Talk with your child about the ideas addressed in the story.

• Discuss each illustration, mentioning the characters, where they are, and what they are doing.

• Read with expression, pointing to each word. You may want to read the whole story through and then revisit parts of the story to ensure that the meanings of words or phrases are understood.

• Talk about why the character did what he or she did and what your child would do in that situation.

• Help your child connect with characters and events in the story.

Remember, reading with your child should be fun, not forced. Each moment spent reading with your child is a priceless investment in his or her literacy life.

Gail Saunders-Smith, Ph.D.

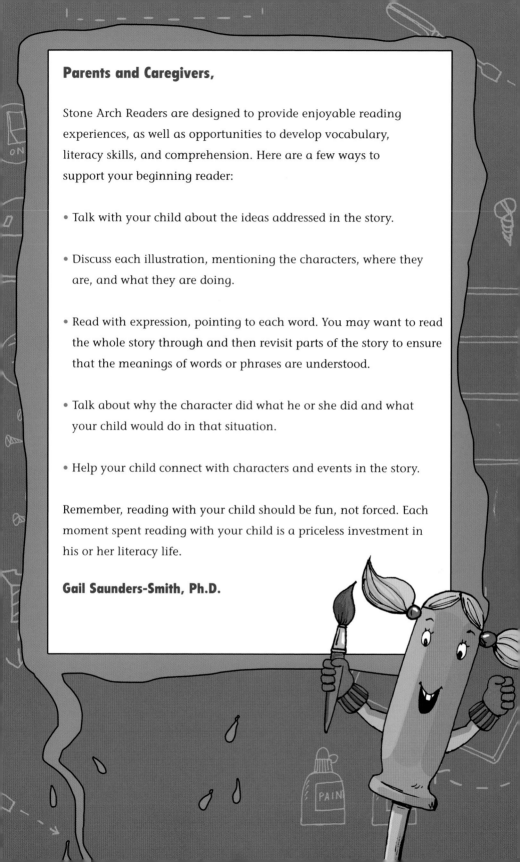

Stone Arch Readers

are published by Stone Arch Books
a Capstone Imprint
1710 Roe Crest Drive
North Mankato, Minnesota 56003
www.capstonepub.com

Library of Congress Cataloging-in-Publication Data
Klein, Adria F. (Adria Fay), 1947-
   Sophie Screwdriver and the classroom / by Adria Klein ; illustrated by Andrew Rowland.
      p. cm. -- (Stone Arch readers--tool school)
   Summary: Sophie Screwdriver and the Tool Team fix up the classroom.
   ISBN 978-1-4342-4021-7 (library binding) -- ISBN 978-1-4342-4235-8 (pbk.)
   1. Screwdrivers--Juvenile fiction. 2. Tools--Juvenile fiction. 3. Classrooms--Juvenile fiction.
4. Helping behavior--Juvenile fiction. [1. Screwdrivers--Fiction. 2. Tools--Fiction. 3. Classrooms--
Fiction. 4. Helpfulness--Fiction.] I. Rowland, Andrew, 1962- ill. II. Title.

   PZ7.K678324Som 2012
   [E]--dc23
                              2011049285

Reading Consultants:
Gail Saunders-Smith, Ph.D.
Melinda Melton Crow, M.Ed.
Laurie K. Holland, Media Specialist

Designer: Russell Griesmer

Printed in China
032012
006677RRDF12

Sophie
Screwdriver
and the Classroom

by Adria Klein   illustrated by Andy Rowland

Sammy Saw

Sophie Screwdriver

The Tool Team meets every day after school. Today, Sophie has a new job for them.

"What's going on, Sophie?"
asks Hank.

Sophie jumps up and down. She twirls around.

"The school needs our help," says Sophie. "Our classroom is a mess."

"Let's get going," says Tia.

"Back to school," says Hank.

"Hurry! Hurry! Hurry! There is
so much to do!" shouts Sophie.

"Calm down, Sophie," says
Hank. "The Tool Team is ready
to work."

"Here's the list," says Sophie.

"Wow! That's a big list," says Sammy.

"Don't worry," says Hank. "If
we work as a team, we'll get it
done."

"Number one," says Hank.
"Change batteries in the clock."

"I'll get the batteries," says Tia.

"And I'll tighten the cover," says
Sophie. "Turn, turn, turn. Job
number one is all done."

"Number two," says Sammy.
"Fix the shelf on the bookcase."

"I'll measure between the shelf
and the top of the bookcase,"
says Tia.

"I will hold it up," says Hank.

"And I will screw it in tight,"
says Sophie. "Turn, turn,
turn. Job number two is all
through."

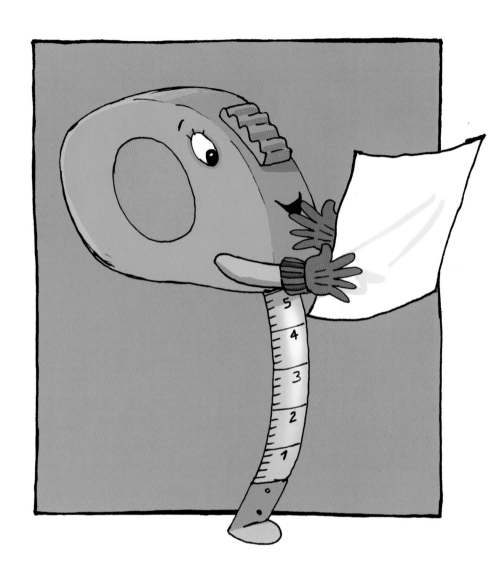

"Number three," says Tia. "Fix the door on the paint cabinet."

"I'll hold it up," says Sammy.

"And I'll screw it in place," says
Sophie. "Turn, turn, turn. Job
number three is done you see."

"Just one more job to do,"
says Sophie.

"What is it?" asks Sammy.

"Hang the new bulletin board,"
says Hank.

"We will have to work together,"
says Tia.

"I will measure the wall," says Tia.

"We will hold the bulletin board,"
says Hank and Sammy.

"And I will screw it in place,"
says Sophie.

"Turn, turn, turn. Job number four
is our final chore," says Sophie.

"Not quite," says Hank.

"What's left?" asks Sophie.

"We need to clean up our mess," says Hank.

"You're right," says Sophie.

The Tool Team cleans and cleans.

"All of our work is finally done.
Let's go and have some fun,"
says Sophie.

"Hooray!" the Tool Team shouts.

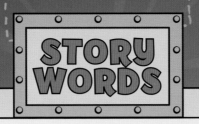

STORY WORDS

list

number

batteries

shelf

Total Word Count: 327

TOOL SCHOOL